The Big W

What were we talking about? Oh yeah, ~~leaving~~ home, the sad day when my mom decided that it was time for me to go out into the world and find myself. Well, I did. Exactly thirty minutes after I left home and went out into the big wide world, I found myself.

Everywhere I went, THERE I WAS! So with that out of the way, I decided to go back home.

When they talk about "the big wide world," they're not kidding. The world outside our yard was bigger and wider than I ever dreamed. It was HUGE. Houses, streets, stores, cars, trees, shrubs, flowers, sidewalks, mailboxes, people.

I saw a bunch of dogs out there, too. Most of them were bigger than me, and most of them looked like they wanted to fight. I did some figuring. If I fought every dog in Twitchell, I would be 127 years old and really messed up. Is that what Mom wanted me to do with my life? I didn't think so.

So I dug a tunnel under the fence and sneaked back in to the yard.

Drover's
Secret Life

John R. Erickson

Illustrations by Gerald L. Holmes

Maverick Books, Inc.

MAVERICK BOOKS, INC.
Published by Maverick Books, Inc.
P.O. Box 549, Perryton, TX 79070
Phone: 806.435.7611
www.hankthecowdog.com

First published in the United States of America by Viking Children's Books and
Puffin Books (simultaneously), members of Penguin Putnam Books for Young
Readers, 2009.
Currently published by Maverick Books, Inc., 2014

1 3 5 7 9 10 8 6 4 2

LIBRARY OF CONGRESS CATALOGING-IN-PUBLICATION DATA
Erickson, John R., 1943–
Hank the Cowdog : Drover's secret life / by Drover C. Dog
[John R. Erickson ; illustrated by Gerald L. Holmes].
p. cm.—(Hank the Cowdog ; #53)
Summary: Drover C. Dog—faithful sidekick to Hank the Cowdog—tells the story
of his life, from being the runt of the litter with dreams of being a handsome
prince, to how he came to Loper and Sally May's ranch.
ISBN978-1-59188-153-7
[1. Dogs—Fiction. 2. Authorship—Fiction. 3. Mothers and sons—Fiction.
4. Texas—Fiction. 5. Humorous stories.] I. Holmes, Gerald L., ill. II. Title.
PZ7.E72556Hao 2009   [Fic]—dc22

Maverick Books, Inc. ISBN 978-1-59188-153-7

To Janee McCartor, who takes care of Hank and Drover at Maverick Books.

The Names and Numbers of All My Chapters

Introduction

It's me again, Hank the Cowdog. Have you ever wondered what Drover does when he runs to the machine shed and hides? I've wondered about that, many times. I mean, the little mutt spends a lot of time in there. What does he do?

I asked him about it one time, and he said, "I count goats."

"Goats? Why do you count goats? We don't even have goats on this ranch."

"Well, if I counted sheep, I might fall asleep. When you sleep, everything's dark and I'm scared of the dark."

Does that make sense to you? It made no sense to me, but over the years I've learned . . . how can I say this? I've learned not to expect much from Drover's answers. All we can say is that he spends a lot of time in the machine shed and sometimes he counts goats that don't exist.

But guess what. That isn't all he does in there. I recently discovered that the little goof has been *writing his life's story*. You think I'm kidding? I'm not kidding. He scratched it out in the dust on the machine-shed floor. I found it just the other day, half an acre of chicken scratch in the dirt.

Naturally, my first thought was that it should be erased at once. I mean, it was written by the same guy who hides under his gunnysack bed and snaps at snowflakes. Is the world ready to face an entire book about his life? No, and without a moment's hesitation, I . . .

You know, I couldn't bring myself to erase it. In fact, I started reading and . . . well, it was weird but also pretty funny. I laughed until my ribs hurt. It was so very . . . Drover.

I'm not saying that the world is ready for it or that you should read it, but if you want to give it a peek, here it is. If it causes you to count goats or snap at snowflakes, don't blame me.

—Hank

This Is the First Chapter

Well, let's see here. How should I start this? I've never done this before and I'm kind of nervous. What if I mess up? Everybody might laugh and I'd hate that.

Most dogs go through their whole life without writing a book, and so have I up to now, but all at once I feel an urge to write an exciting story about the life of Drover C. Dog.

That's me. If I'm going to be an author, I need a name that sounds like something an author might use. Plain old "Drover" doesn't sound very exciting, does it? I don't think so. "Drover C. Dog" sounds more dramatic. It's the kind of name that needs trumpets or something.

I made it up myself. I used "Dog" as my last

name because . . . well, I'm a dog and it fits. The middle initial "C" just came out of thin air.

That's a funny way of putting it, "thin air." Is there some other kind of air? I don't know, it all seems pretty thin to me, otherwise we'd choke when we tried to breathe.

You can choke on water, I know that. I saw a bat almost drown one time. It was a hot day and he needed a drink, but he fell in a goldfish pond because he was half-blind and he couldn't swim. I had to drag him out. His name was Boris O'Bat and he'll come up later in the story, if I get that far. I'm not sure I will. If I don't . . . well, I saved a bat once and it was kind of exciting.

I picked *C* as my middle initial. It seemed as good as any and, besides, I've always wanted to see the ocean . . . see the sea, you might say, and all at once everything fit together: *C,* see, and sea.

It's neat when things fit together like that, so my writer-name is going to be Drover C. Dog. One of these days maybe we'll see it in lights.

There's that word again, *see.* It just keeps popping up. Maybe my new name will bring me good luck. I hope so. Bad luck is not so good and I don't need any of that.

Anyway, I'm kind of nervous. I want this to be a good story, not something boring. That'll be a challenge. Hank tells me that I'm pretty boring and I have a feeling that he's right.

But just because you're a boring little mutt doesn't mean you have to write a boring story. I'll try to make it exciting, but not right now. Just this little bit of writing has worn me out and I need a nap. See you in an hour.

The Next Day

That turned into a pretty long nap, about fifteen hours of wonderful doggie sleep. I dreamed about . . . I don't remember, but it was a great dream. Now I'm fresh and wide awake and I have to start the story of my secret life.

Here we go.

Okay, I was born and that's how it all began. Then I grew up and here I am and not much happened in between.

Hank was right. My life has been so boring, even I can't stand to hear about it. I'm a failure as a writer. I knew I would be. I'm so embarrassed! Good-bye.

The Next Day

Well, I'm back. I'm not going to quit. Just because you have nothing to say doesn't mean you shouldn't write about it. And besides, I *have* something to say. I thought of it last night in my sleep.

Here we go again.

Like I said, I was born and that's how it all began. Mom said I was there but I don't remember. All I know is what she told me. One day she was sitting in the yard when all at once she got an urge to go camping. She thought that was odd because she'd never cared for camping. She scouted around the yard until she found an empty box and some rags for bedding.

She said camping was fun but it gave her indigestion. She thought it was indigestion, but when my brother Willie was born, she knew something was up.

I was number nine, the last pup to hit the ground. Mom said that when she saw me, she screamed, "This isn't funny! All I did was go camping and now I'm sharing a box with nine wet rats!"

It took her a while to figure out that those "wet rats" were her own children and she'd just taken a full-time job as a mother. She thought we were the ugliest things she'd ever seen, but after she cried for a while, she licked us dry and served lunch.

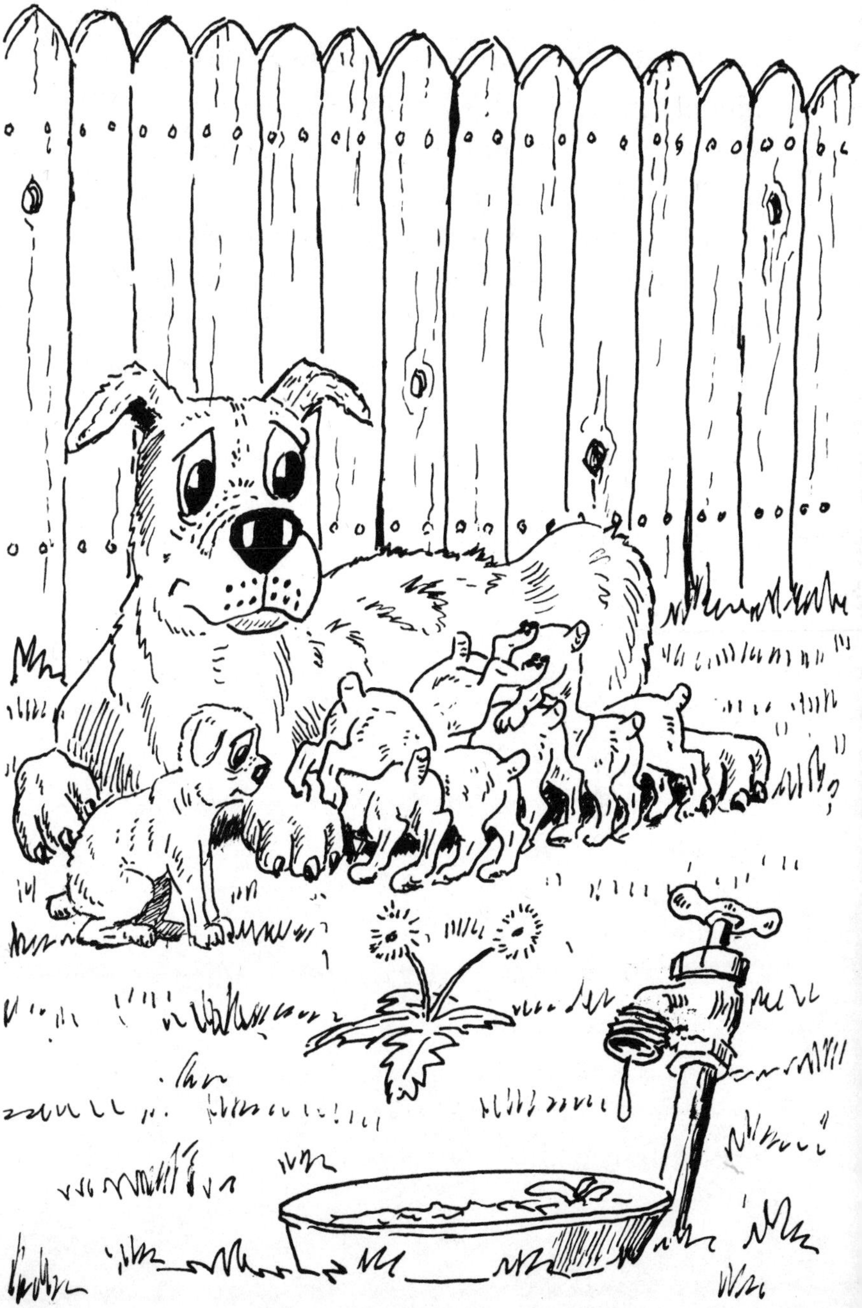

Like I said, there were nine of us and she only had eight plates at her table. Willie and I had to share a plate. He always went first and ate like a pig. I got what was left.

Well, those are my earliest memories . . . or they would be if I could remember that far back but I can't.

A Sad and Lonely Childhood

Here's a secret, if you promise not to tell: *My childhood wasn't so bad.* In fact I had a good life. But who wants to read about some dog who's had a happy childhood? Nobody.

That's why I called this chapter "A Sad and Lonely Childhood." When you write about being happy, everybody falls asleep.

But back to my brother, Willie. There were nine of us pups but only eight plates at Mom's table, so Willie and I had to share, and he ate like a pig. He grew up to be big and strong, and I grew up to be a runt with a stub tail.

We lived in a fenced yard in the town of Twitchell, Texas. That's kind of a funny name, Twitchell. I was always the smallest dog in a crowd and scared of everything. You name it, I was scared of it: storms, loud noises, water, the dark. My brothers barked at cars. Not me. I hid in the bushes. Some of the dogs in the neighborhood chewed up newspapers, but I didn't. I was always scared I'd choke on the rubber band.

Some of my friends barked at the mailman when he walked his route every day, and they said it was gobs of fun. I never tried it. He carried a big leather bag on his shoulder, and I was scared that if I barked at him, he'd stuff me in that bag and carry me off to someplace awful.

I didn't know where he came from or where he went after he left the mail, and I didn't want to find out. I always thought there was something a little fishy about those postal employees, so I stayed away from them.

I wasn't proud of being a little chicken. Dogs should be brave and do courageous things. That's what everybody says. I dreamed of being brave and fighting monsters, but the older I grew, the chickener I got.

You know, maybe my childhood wasn't as happy as I thought, 'cause I spent a lot of time being scared and worrying about my tail. One day Mom and I had a talk.

She said, "Well, son, your brothers and sisters

have all grown up and moved away."

"Yeah, it gets lonesome sometimes."

"Not lonesome. Peaceful."

"I kind of miss 'em, but there's more to eat now that they're gone."

"Which brings up a touchy subject."

"I don't miss Willie, the greedy pig."

"Hello?" She waved a paw in front of my eyes. "Did you hear anything I just said?"

"Oh, hi Mom. Did you say something?"

"Yes. I had just brought up a touchy subject. You."

"Gosh, I didn't know I was a touchy subject."

"Drover, there comes a time in a dog's life when he needs to move along."

"Yeah, but that's after he grows up."

"That's the point. In people-years, you're twenty-five years old. And you're still hanging around the yard. It's starting to embarrass me. Does it embarrass you?"

"Let me think. Nope."

"Well, it should. I see dogs in the neighborhood whispering."

"Yeah, I've wondered why they whisper all the time."

"They're gossiping about YOU. They're wondering if you're ever going to grow up. And you know what?" She looked into my eyes. "So am I."

"Well, I've tried, Mom, and it just hasn't worked. So I guess I'll stick around for a while, if that's okay."

"It's not okay. Your brothers and sisters have their own homes now, and jobs. And you . . . what are you going to do, be a bum?"

"Would you mind?"

"You'd be a bum? You'd actually do that to your poor mother?"

"Well, I've thought about it."

"You will *not* be a bum!" All at once a look of deep concern came into her face. She leaned toward me and whispered, "Drover, what's wrong with you? You can tell me, I'm your mother."

All my life I'd tried to hide the shame, but now she was asking for the truth. "It's my tail, Mom."

"What's wrong with your tail? I like your tail."

"I hate my tail. It's just a stub."

"Don't call it a stub. You make it sound like a handicap."

"It *is* a handicap."

"Drover, it's called a 'docked tail' and it's like a haircut for dogs. It improves your appearance and gives you a tidy look."

"It used to be twice as long and now it's twice as short."

"It looks twice as good."

"I hate it twice as much."

She rolled her eyes. "Never mind your tail. What else is wrong with you?"

"I'm a runt."

"You're not a runt. You're small."

"A dog knows, Mom. I'm a runt."

"Okay, you're a runt, so what?"

"I'm a runt with a sawed-off tail."

"Honey, the world needs runts. For every runt, there's a job looking for a runt."

"Like what?

"You know the list: bird dog, guard dog, stock dog, leader dog, tracking dog, house dog, yard dog, porch dog. So, what'll it be?"

"I have to decide right now?"

"I'll give you two minutes, and being a bum isn't an option. Choose something respectable."

I thought about it, then revealed my secret dream. "Mom, ever since I was a little guy, I've wanted to be a handsome prince."

Her mouth dropped open, and for a whole minute she couldn't speak. "A handsome prince? That's a job? Do you need training?"

"I don't know. Maybe there's a Handsome Prince School somewhere."

She turned away and shook her head. "Oi yoi yoi! But you'll move out of the yard, right?"

"Well, you know, I was thinking . . ."

"You'll move out of the yard. If they're not hiring princes, try pointing birds, anything. And son, always remember . . ."

"Okay."

"I haven't said it yet."

"Oh. Sorry."

"Always remember, my son, it's not the size of the dog in the fight that matters."

"Yeah, I've heard it a thousand times. It's the size of the bog in the fog."

She stared at me for a long moment. "For you, that's close enough."

"Thanks, Mom. You always know what to say."

"Really? Ha ha ha!" For some reason she walked away, laughing like crazy. Me? I left home and went out into the world to find myself.

And that's the story of my sad and lonely childhood. Like I said, it wasn't all that sad and lonely, but I did spend some time worrying about my tail.

Alone in a Cold World

~~~~~~

You know, it's kind of funny. Living here on the ranch, I've noticed that it turns cold in the wintertime, and it happens every year. You can almost predict it. I think it has something to do with Halloween.

Before Halloween, the days are warm and sunny. But then the birds leave and I've never understood why they do that. All summer they seem happy, chirping and singing and hopping around on their skinny legs and flying through the air.

They seem to enjoy flying through the air, don't they? I would too, if I could fly, but I can't. I tried it once. My friend Pete (he's a cat) told me that if I jumped out of the back of the pickup and wiggled my ears, I could soar like a weevil.

I gave it a try, but mostly I soared straight down and crashed my nose into the ground and it hurt pretty bad. Pete said I didn't do it right, that's why I crashed, and he told me to wiggle the left ear more than the right one.

He boosted up my confidence so much, I felt like Super Dog and tried it again, took a another dive off the back of Slim's pickup. That one hurt too, but Pete was right there at my side when I picked myself up. He'd watched the whole thing, so he told me what I did wrong.

You'll never guess what it was. It was such a tiny little mistake that I never would have noticed, if Pete hadn't told me. *I forgot to press my lips together.* Can you believe that? I felt so silly.

Since this is my secret story, I can admit something. That wasn't the first time in my life that I'd felt dumb. It wasn't the second time either. It's happened a lot. It's never good to go around feeling foolish about yourself. It affects your whole attitude and that's the great thing about having a friend like Pete.

Maybe I shouldn't call him my friend. He's a cat, you know, and I could get in big trouble for saying that I'm friends with a cat. Hank would throw a fit, but it's the truth. Pete is my friend and when I crashed that second time . . . third time . . .

I crashed a whole bunch of times that day. Twenty or twenty-five times. I just couldn't get the hang of flying. Each time, I made some little mistake and I felt sure that Pete would get tired of watching one failure after another and get discouraged and quit helping me, but he didn't.

I got pretty discouraged myself, and even started crying. "Pete, I just can't do it anymore, I can't go on with this. I feel like such a failure!"

I'll never forget his words, they were so touching. He said, "Drover, the only difference between a failure and a hero is . . . one leg's the same."

Gee, I'd never thought of that, and his words went through me like a wooden nickel and gave me hope and courage. With his help, I climbed back into the pickup bed and made another flight.

By the time darkness fell that evening, we had erected a Monument to Dogs in Flight. Pete called it a "Backward Monument" because it didn't stand up like a statue. It went down into the ground, like a hole.

It *was* a hole, the hole my nose had punched into the ground, but like Pete said, by golly, it

was OUR hole, and there it was for everyone to see, a living tribute to brave dogs and their flying machines.

It sure made me proud, seeing that monument. I'd put a lot of myself into making that hole, but I couldn't have done it without Pete's help.

But where was I? Oh, yeah, there's something about Halloween that makes the weather turn cold. That's when monsters come out, too—skeletons and witches and some guy in a helmet named Dark Vader. He wears a black cape and talks like he's got a bad cold and he scares the bejeebers out of me. He comes to the ranch every Halloween.

The first time he came to Loper and Sally May's house, Hank made me go out and bark at him. I didn't want to but I did, gave him one bark and ran like greased lightning to the machine shed.

Hank got mad and called me a chicken liver but I didn't care. Dark Vader came back the next year and I ran for the machine shed again, only this time I didn't bark at him. He keeps coming back every year at Halloween, but we've kind of reached an understanding: I never bark at him and he never eats me. Whenever he comes to the ranch and gets out of the car, I go straight to the machine shed and stay there until he leaves. No muss, no fuss, no noise, no nothing.

I don't know why he keeps coming back on Halloween, but he never seems to do any harm. If he ever tried to hurt anyone or steal something, maybe I'd leave the machine shed and bark at him. Or maybe not. Probably not.

I don't remember what I was talking about when I started this chapter, but I think it's time to start another one. You can't stay in the same chapter forever. If you told your whole life's story in one chapter, it might seem kind of boring.

The next chapter is going to be exciting.

CHAPTER FOUR

The Next Chapter

I need to work on my concentration. It's always been hard for me, thinking about one thing at a time. There's always so much going on.

This ranch sure is a busy place and it's hard to keep my mind on *My Secret Life*. I haven't gotten to the part yet about how I ended up living on Loper and Sally May's ranch, but I'm heading in that direction.

But you know what? I have an itch that won't go away, and I'm going to have to scratch it. I don't want to. I want to keep telling all the great adventures I found after leaving home, but I can't stand this any longer.

Will you wait? I'm sorry, but if I don't scratch

this thing right now, I won't be able to think about anything else. Don't leave.

Scratch scratch scratch!

There! Boy, that was a good one. I feel a lot better and I hope you do, too.

What were we talking about? Oh yeah, leaving home, the sad day when my mom decided that it was time for me to go out into the world and find myself. Well, I did. Exactly thirty minutes after I left home and went out into the big wide world, I found myself.

Everywhere I went, THERE I WAS! So with that out of the way, I decided to go back home.

When they talk about "the big wide world," they're not kidding. The world outside our yard was bigger and wider than I ever dreamed. It was HUGE. Houses, streets, stores, cars, trees, shrubs, flowers, sidewalks, mailboxes, people.

I saw a bunch of dogs out there, too. Most of them were bigger than me, and most of them looked like they wanted to fight. I did some figuring. If I fought every dog in Twitchell, I would be 127 years old and really messed up. Is that what Mom wanted me to do with my life? I didn't think so.

So I dug a tunnel under the fence and sneaked back into the yard. I saw Mom in the distance, lying in the shade and chewing on a soup bone. She wore a radiant smile and I heard her say, "At last, peace and quiet! All the kids grown and gone, and I have a bone all to myself. It's a good life."

I tried to tiptoe across the yard and hide in a patch of flowers, but her ears shot up and the bone rolled out of her mouth. Then her voice ripped through the silence. "Drover! What are you doing back here? I sent you out into the world and here you are, back again!"

"Mom, I tried the world. It's too big and . . ." Right then and there, something happened to my leg, honest. It just . . . terrible pain came shooting up from my toes and before I knew what was happening, I was limping around in circles. "Oh my leg! This thing's killing me!"

At first she seemed suspicious, but as my groans of pain grew louder and my limp got worse and worse, she said, "Well, maybe you should lie down."

"Thanks, Mom. Just one night, that'll fix it. Boy, I don't know what happened, but this thing is really . . . oh, the pain! Oh, my leg!"

A month later, Mom's attitude had gotten really bad. I mean, sour. She'd used all her home remedies and motherly cures but, drat the luck, my leg kept getting worse. I felt awful about it, but what's a dog to do when he gets struck down in the prime of his rib?

One morning she came to my bedside. "How's the leg?"

I tried to hide the pain, the terrible pain, but a groan just popped out of my mouth. "You know, Mom, I thought it was getting better . . . no, I'm *sure* it was getting better, but then it took a turn for the worse. I don't know what to say."

"Which leg?"

"Left front, down in the ankle. Ooooo! Awful pain."

"Yesterday it was the right rear, around the knee."

"It was? No fooling?"

"No fooling."

"Gosh. How do you explain that?"

"I'm wondering."

"Well, I guess the pain is moving around, huh? I've heard about Moving Pain. It's the very worst kind."

"Oh really?"

"Yes, you bet. Last year it took a terrible toll. Dogs all over Texas were dropping like flies."

"Mercy."

"And they say the only cure is lots of rest."

"How much rest are we talking about?"

"Oh . . . months, sometimes years. It just depends."

"I see." Mom walked a few steps away, whirled around all of a sudden, and screamed at the top of her lungs, "DROVER, THE YARD IS ON FIRE!! RUN FOR YOUR LIFE!!"

Well, I'd never been the kind of dog who wanted to mess around with fire. It took only one fire alarm to get me out of bed. I headed straight for the tunnel under the fence and dived in.

Safe on the other side, I yelled, "Come on, Mom, I'll help you through!" Silence. "Mom? Hurry!" I heard a clunking sound coming from inside the hole. "Mom?" I stuck my head back in the hole and saw that the opening had been plugged with a board. "Mom? Hey Mom, you'll have to jump the fence. Somebody plugged the tunnel! Mom?"

I held my breath, hoping the fire hadn't . . .

Finally, she spoke. "Drover?"

"Mom? Thank goodness! Are you all right?"

"I'm fine. Your leg seems better."

My eyes drifted around. "Well, not really. I mean, it was okay there for a minute, but now the pain's coming back. Maybe I'd better lie down."

"Not in my yard."

"What?"

"I said, can you come for Christmas dinner?"

"Christmas dinner? Mom, that's six months from now. Mom? Hello?"

What can you say when your own mother locks you out of the yard? It's about the saddest story I ever heard. Even today it brings mist to my eyes.

CHAPTER FIVE

I Never Got to
Be Joe

I woke up this morning on my gunnysack under the gas tanks, thinking about that Monument to Dogs in Flight, and I'm sure glad I woke up. Otherwise I'd still be asleep.

I enjoy sleeping. I love to sleep. I'd rather sleep than do almost anything, but I wouldn't want to do it all the time, day and night. I think I'd get tired of it after a while.

If you get tired of running, you can always lie down and sleep, but if you get tired of lying down and sleeping, what do you do? I worry about things like that.

I worry about a lot of stuff. What would happen if the sun didn't come up in the morning? What if it came up in the evening? How would we know if it was evening or morning?

It would mess up everything. Here at the ranch, Sally May brings out the breakfast scraps right after breakfast, which is in the morning. If the sun came up in the evening, would breakfast still be breakfast or would we have to call it something else? What would we call it?

I've thought of a good name for it: Joe. It's easy to spell and I've always liked the name Joe. When I was a pup, I wanted to be Joe but I couldn't because I was Drover, and also there was already some dog named Joe. I never met him, but why couldn't we have two Joes in the world?

I asked Mom about that when I was young, but she didn't have a good answer. All she said was, "Drover, I worry about you." Well, if she was so worried about me, how come she locked me out of the yard and told me to get a job?

What did I know about a job? I was just a poor scared kid with a stub tail, a pup who'd always dreamed of being a Joe but couldn't be.

I never noticed this before, but if you take the word J-O-E, drop the *E* and add *B,* you get J-O-B. That seems pretty significant. B = bee, and we had some bees in our back yard. If a bee stung

JOE, the *E* might fall off and you'd have J-O-Bee. Get it? J-O-B.

No wonder I was afraid of getting a job. That explains it, 'cause I've always been scared of bees.

I have to admit, I wasn't exactly a kid when Mom locked me out of the yard. I was almost grown. All my brothers and sisters had moved out and found new homes, even Willie, the greedy pig. So maybe I was too old to be living at home, but just because you're too old doesn't mean you weren't a kid at some point in your life.

Everybody has to be something. Otherwise what would we do?

It really hurt my feelings when Mom locked me out of the yard. There I was, a runt with a stub tail, a dog who'd always wanted to be named Joe but couldn't be. That right there was enough to break anyone's heart, but on top of that I had a serious medical condition, *Leggus Brokus* with Moving Pain Syndrome.

And she locked me out of the yard and wondered if I could come back for Christmas dinner!

Christmas dinner! By Christmas, I would be skin and bones. I would look exactly like what's left of a Christmas turkey after Christmas dinner.

Who would offer a job to a turkey carcass with a stub tail?

Real turkeys don't have stub tails. They have feathers and they're really pretty when they fan them out, but if you're a dog, you can never be a turkey. No matter how many times you wish upon a star, you'll be a dog until you wither away to skin and bones, and then you're still a dog, only you'll look like a turkey carcass the day after Christmas.

Anyway, I woke up this morning thinking about the Monument to Dogs in Flight. You know what? All at once it doesn't seem like much of a monument: a hole in the ground. I know, Pete said it was a Backward Monument and a tribute to my heroic efforts to fly, and I went to a lot of trouble to build it. But still . . .

The hole is still there and somehow it just looks ridiculous. Just a hole in the ground. A monument should make somebody proud of something, but every time I look at that hole, it makes me remember all those times I flapped my ears and dove off the back of the pickup and landed nose-first on the ground.

It doesn't make me proud. It makes me wonder . . . how come, after I had the first wreck, I climbed back up there and did it a second time? And before I can answer that question, I find myself wondering, "Gosh, how come I did it the third time?" And it gets worse from there. I crashed twenty-five times. That's why the hole is so deep.

Something's not right.

An Ugly Scene
with Mom

Here we are in Chapter Six. I kind of wish it was Chapter Seven, then I could call it "Chapter Crutch." See, the shape of a 7 reminds me of a crutch.

Back when I was living in the yard with Mom, my leg gave me so much misery that I might have used a crutch, if I'd had one. But I didn't have a crutch and this isn't Chapter Seven, so I can't call it "Chapter Crutch."

Here at the ranch, we had a pretty wild time last night. Big storm, thunder, lightning, crash, boom, and little green Charlie Monsters running all over the place, trying to invade the ranch. Hank went out to bark at the Charlies.

I tried to follow. I really wanted to go but, drat the luck, the old leg quit me just when Hank called for the attack. I went down like a rock, flat on my back, in terrible pain. Hank wasn't very sympathetic, and I couldn't blame him. It happens every time.

Almost every time.

Every time.

Hank thinks I need surgery. Brain surgery, is what he said. I'm not sure what he meant, but I'm not keen on having an operation. Everything in a hospital is white and I don't like white. It seems colorless. I guess it is colorless. That's what makes it white.

Maybe I ought to go to a chiropractor. They have chiropractors for dogs, and I've heard that after a couple of adjustments, your backbone straightens out and gets longer. I'm not sure that would help my leg, but it might longerate my tail. I'm still self-conscious about my tail.

It's always something—my leg, my tail, allergies. By doze geds stobbed ub all the tibe. See what I bean? All I have to do is thig abou dit.

Anyway, after Mom locked me out of the yard, I had to do something drastic—either suck up my courage and go look for a job, or sit there and moan about it for the rest of my life and feel sorry for myself. That didn't leave me much of a choice, did it? Nope. And it didn't take me long to swing into action.

Right then and there, I made up my mind to moan and howl until Mom let me back in the yard. Boy, it was tough. I mean all day and half the night, hours of the saddest moaning and howling you ever heard. Mom didn't respond, which surprised me. I thought she'd gone deaf or moved out, but finally, around three o'clock in the morning, she spoke through a crack in the fence.

"Drover?"

"Hi, Mom, how's it going?"

"Son, there are two words I've never wanted to use in your presence."

"I'll be derned. Am I supposed to guess?"

"No. Just listen. The words are 'shut' and 'up.'"

"'Shut and up'?"

"Say it fast."

"Shutandup?"

"Drover, take out the 'and' and say it fast."

"Oh, okay. Shut up! Oops. Mom, I can't believe I said that. It just slipped out, honest."

"Don't apologize. It was meant for *you*."

"For me? You're telling me to shut up?"

"Yes. You've finally done it. You've pushed me

into using harsh language and made me sound like a hag. Are you happy?"

"I don't think so. How about you?"

"Who can be happy with you out there, moaning like a lost calf?"

"Oh good, you noticed."

"Of course I noticed! Everyone in the neighborhood noticed. That's why, for the past six hours, they've been yelling at you."

"Gosh, someone's been yelling at me?"

"Only the whole neighborhood."

"No fooling? Hey, here's an idea. Let me back in the yard and we'll talk about it."

"No! Get a job and we'll talk about it . . . at Christmas."

"Mom, I can't. Nobody would hire a little mutt who moans all night long."

"So stop moaning!"

"Well . . . it's kind of fun, to be honest. And I don't have anything better to do."

"You think it's fun? Listen, buster, keep it up and somebody's going to call the dogcatcher."

"Dogcatcher? Who'd do a thing like that?"

"Fifteen people who can't sleep."

"Oh, surely not. That would be mean."

"I guess you can try it and find out."

"Maybe I will. It beats looking for a job. Hee hee."

"Some dogs never learn. Well, good night and good luck."

"Good night, Mom. If you change your mind, I'll be right here."

I couldn't believe she was being so unreasonable. And stubborn. All I wanted was to move back home for the rest of my life. Was that asking too much?

This Is
Pretty Neat

Well, we finally made it to Chapter Seven, and did you see what I called it? "Chapter Crutch." Hee hee. It was fun.

And you know what else? When we get to Chapter Eight, I might call it "Chapter Train Tracks," and I'll bet you can't guess why. Go ahead and try. In a thousand years, you won't guess.

Give up?

Here on the ranch, Little Alfred has a model train set with the track glued on a sheet of plywood and the track follows the pattern of a figure 8. Eight reminds me of his train tracks. Is that neat or what?

Every now and then I get a kick out of doing

something wild and rebellious. Sometimes it scares me. Two days ago when Hank said "Good morning," I stuck out my tongue at him. No reason. I just felt a crazy urge to do it and I did it.

He was shocked and so was I, and he made me stand in the corner for ten minutes. It was worth it, and one of these days I'll do it again.

I still haven't gotten to the part about how I found a home here on Loper and Sally May's ranch, but I'm working my way in that direction.

Anyway, Alfred's train track is too big to keep in the house all the time, so they store it in the machine shed. I know every square inch of that machine shed and everything inside it. That's where I go when life becomes unbearable, which happens fairly often.

Sometimes it's caused by a major event: a storm with lots of thunder and lightning; a can of hair spray blowing up in the garbage barrel when the cowboys burn trash; Hank getting in trouble with Sally May and getting flogged by her broom.

That happens pretty often around here, Hank getting crossways with Sally May. She's a nice lady and I get along with her, but she and Hank . . . wow. They strike sparks. If you ask me, getting along with Sally May isn't all that hard. She has her rules and all you have to do is follow them.

1. Stay out of her yard and leave her flowers alone.

2. Don't lick her on the ankles. She hates that.

3. If you get sick and throw up, don't eat it again while she's around. It really grosses her out.

4. Don't wet on her car tires. The cowboys don't care if we mark their pickup tires. They don't even notice, but Sally May always notices and it always makes her mad.

5. Don't pick fights with her cat. Hank thinks Pete's a little sneak and most of the time he's right about that, but being right and winning don't always happen at the same time around here.

Hank doesn't follow Sally May's rules and he gets in trouble every time—not every *other* time, but every time. He never seems to learn, but I have that problem myself, so who am I to talk? Does it have something to do with being a dog? I've wondered about that.

Anyway, I hide in the machine shed to get

away from explosions, arguments, loud noises, and things that are scary. But sometimes I go there for other reasons, like feeling guilty.

I spend a lot of time feeling guilty and it really drags me down. I get to thinking about all the things I could be and should be . . . and would be, if it wasn't so much trouble, and boy howdy, the guilt just starts piling up.

It bothers me that I'm not as brave as I ought to be. That's a real problem when you're supposed to be guarding a ranch. I worry about that a lot, and I don't know how many times I've made the decision to work on my courage.

The trouble is that working on a problem is *work* and . . . well, I get tired and discouraged and the old leg starts to throb, and before I know it, I'm just eaten up with guilt.

But there's always hope and help in the machine shed, and a couple of hours in there usually takes care of it. Sometimes it takes longer, but for ordinary guilt attacks, two hours will fix me up. Then I can go right back to doing what I always dreamed of doing: not much.

But maybe I'd better get back to the story. We're fixing to come to the exciting part. I can hardly wait.

The Exciting Part

Mom was right. One of the neighbors called the dogcatcher on me. Boy, was that a shock. Here's what happened.

There I was out in the alley, moaning and howling, when all at once a pickup stopped right beside me. I didn't think anything about it, but this man stepped out and came toward me, holding a net with a wooden handle.

I thought maybe he was collecting butterflies. Some people do that. Why not? They're pretty. I enjoy looking at butterflies myself.

I stopped moaning and gave him a friendly smile, as if to say, "Oh hi. Looking for butterflies? I saw one yesterday, yellow with black spots."

As he came closer, I noticed that he looked

pretty serious. If a guy was out catching butterflies, he'd be having fun. He wasn't having fun, and it was the middle of the night. It didn't add up.

He raised the net over his head and swung. I seemed to be right in the way, so I jumped and gave him another friendly smile that said, "Hey, you almost caught me instead of the butterfly."

He raised the net and swung again, and I really had to scramble to get out of the way. It seemed to make him mad and he yelled, "Hold still, will you!"

Hold still? Was he talking to the butterfly or me? I glanced around and didn't see any butterflies. Just then, I heard Mom's voice through the fence. "Drover? What's all the noise out there?"

"Oh, hi, Mom. Well, there's a man out here catching butterflies and I'm trying to help."

WHOP! I jumped out of the way of the net.

Mom said, "What makes you think he's trying to catch butterflies?"

"Well, he's got a net and what else would he be doing?"

WHOP!

"Ninny! I tried to warn you. That's the dogcatcher, and he's trying to catch *you*!"

"Me?" WHOP! "Hey Mom, what if he catches me? What then?"

"He'll take you to Devil's Island for Dogs."

"Devil's Island? That doesn't sound good."

"That's why I told you to quit making all that racket, but do you ever listen to your mother? No. Now look at you!"

WHOP!

"Hey Mom, I think he's serious. What should I do?"

She raised her voice to a screech. "What do you think you should do? Run!"

"Yeah, but this leg . . ."

"Stop yapping and run!"

You know, it was kind of a miracle. All at once the pain that had tormented me for so many days and weeks just floated away, and I was running like a silver streak down the alley. Deep inside, I felt that I could keep it up for, oh, fifty yards before the leg went out again.

But yipes, the dogcatcher didn't quit after fifty yards. He stayed right on my tail, swinging the net and yelling about all the terrible things he was going to do when he caught me, and somehow that inspired me to keep chugging along. Lucky for me, the old leg stayed with me.

I kept thinking he'd get tired and quit, but on and on we went—down the alley, up a street, and down another alley. Before long, I was lost—lost and scared and worn out. I couldn't go another step. I figured this was IT, I was cooked.

That's when I heard a mysterious voice. It came out of nowhere and said, "Drover, is that you?"

I looked all around and didn't see anyone . . . well, I saw the dogcatcher coming down the alley. He looked as tired as me—hair down in his face, puffing for air, dragging his net, and very mad, but still coming toward me. The voice I'd heard hadn't come from him.

You know, in a lot of stories, when the main character gets into trouble and things are looking dark, he runs into a Mysterious Stranger who pops up out of nowhere and rescues him from danger. Did you notice that "stranger" rhymes with "danger"? It does and sometimes that's an important sign.

So I said, "Hello, voice? You must be a Mysterious Stranger. Listen, my mother locked me out of the yard, and there's an angry dogcatcher coming after me and I really need to be rescued."

"Drover, is that you?"

"Yes, but I can't believe you know my name. This is really magic!"

"It's not magic."

"Yeah, but you knew my name and you can't even see me."

"I'm your mother."

I looked closer at the yard fence and realized that I'd gone in a big circle. "Mom? It's really you? Can we talk?"

"We've talked! How much talk does it take?"

"Well, this time it's kind of important. Do you want your son to be a jailbird? The dogcatcher's after me."

She let out a groan. "All right, one more time."

She moved the board. I dived into the tunnel and came up inside the yard, then held my breath and hoped that the dogcatcher hadn't seen me. His footsteps went past and down the alley.

I almost fainted with relief. "Thanks, Mom. Gee, it's great to be back home."

"One night, that's it, no more."

"Thanks, Mom, you won't regret this."

"I already do. Go to bed. Sleep. Tomorrow, you're gone."

"Good night, Mom."

"I can't believe this."

The next morning she came to wake me up but couldn't find me. Hee hee. It was a big yard and I was hiding in a shrub. She thought I'd gotten myself out of bed and gone off to look for a job. She was so proud, I didn't have the heart to show myself.

It was pretty awkward, to tell you the truth, and it got worse with every passing day. I stayed hidden during the day and came out at night to eat. She began to notice the empty dog food bowl. "Did I eat all that? I'm going to be as big as a house."

But then she started getting suspicious and thought some of the neighborhood cats were stealing her food. I kind of played along with that. After I was done eating, I'd meow like a cat and it sure worked. Hee hee.

But then she caught me hiding in the bush. Boy, she threw a fit. "You again!"

"Hi Mom. Surprise."

"You're not a cat."

"Thanks, and neither are you."

"Hush. I thought you left days ago."

"Well, I almost did, but it seemed like a lot of trouble."

"I'll show you trouble." She stuck her nose in my face. "Out. Now. Go find a job."

"So sudden?"

"This isn't sudden. It's been going on for months. Go!"

With a heavy heart, I made my way to the tunnel under the fence. I'd used up all my tricks, and it appeared that I was really getting kicked out this time. Only she took her eyes off me for a couple of seconds, and I hid behind a wheelbarrow when she wasn't looking. Hee hee. It was pretty sneaky.

For a couple of days I hid behind the wheelbarrow. I had plenty of time to think about the future and getting a job and all that other stuff, and I even composed a song about it. No fooling. I think it was pretty good. You want to hear it?

I Have No Ambition

I have no ambition.
I'm not on a mission.
I'd rather go fishin'
Than look for a job.

But Mother's a cheapskate
And now she is irate.
She thinks I'll be jail bait
If I'm unemployed.

    I think I will throw up,
    I don't want to grow up,

I don't want to show up
For job interviews.

My life would be easier
With nothing but leisure.
I never will please her,
So what is the point?

She thinks I'm a bum.
I know that it's dumb.
I'm sucking my thumb
And trying to hide.

I'd rather stay home
And sit like a stone
Or chew on a bone
Or sleep in the shade.

Nobody would hire me.
I'm sure they would fire me.
The effort would tire me
And stir up my leg.

There's no sense in wishin'
For nuclear fission.
I have no ambition,
So leave me alone.

CHAPTER NINE

The Bat

That's the best song I ever wrote. It really gets deep into my heart and soul, but I probably shouldn't have sung it so loud. Mom heard me and found my hiding place, and she really blew a gasket. She screamed so loud, she started coughing and couldn't scream any more, or even talk, so she moved out of the yard and started staying on the front porch, and I had the whole backyard to myself.

The weather had been hot and dry for weeks, and one afternoon the temperature climbed up around a hundred thousand degrees. Maybe it was just a hundred degrees, but it felt like a hundred thousand. A locust droned in a tree, and heat waves danced on the horizon, and there wasn't a breath of wind.

It was around the middle of August, and every

dog in town had crawled into the shade of a bush. Nothing moved or stirred in the awful heat. I was shaded up beneath some morning-glory vines, panting in the heat and listening to the water dripping off my tongue.

I was thirsty and could see the little goldfish pond on the other side of the yard, but I couldn't work up the energy to jack myself up, walk all the way over to it, and lap some water. It seemed like a lot of trouble, way too much trouble on such a hot day.

All at once a bird fell out of a tree and landed in the yard. That seemed pretty strange. Birds don't fall out of trees very often, so I watched. This was a funny-looking bird. He had wings but no feathers. I'd never seen a naked bird before.

He pushed himself up off the ground, gave his head a shake, and blinked his eyes. He saw the little pond and started walking toward it, dragging his wings.

Most dogs would have barked. Most dogs don't allow birds in their yards. Me? I didn't give a rip. I was so hot, I didn't care.

He staggered up to the pond, raised a wing above his head, and shouted in a squeaky little voice, "Oh yes! The Colorado River!" Then he stumbled and fell face-first into the pond.

I waited for him to swim or climb out of the pond, but all he did was thrash and squeak. I thought to myself, "This can't be good. Birds need air, like the rest of us. If he doesn't do something, he's going to drown."

I even gave a thought to helping him, but, well, it was *his* life. If he wanted to drown himself in the pond, that was his business. We had about a billion birds in Twitchell, and losing one of them wouldn't exactly be a tragedy.

But I couldn't just sit there. I had to do something. I struggled to my feet and walked out into the glare of the sun. Finally I reached the pond. It just about wore me out. I reached a paw into the water and scooped him out and set him on the ground.

There he lay, gasping and sputtering and flopping his wings. That was some kind of ugly bird. Like I said, no feathers ... and, my gosh, he had huge ears and a pug nose and ... *that was no bird*.

It was a BAT!

I didn't hang around. Bats and I have nothing to say to each other. I don't like bats. I'm scared of bats. They drink blood.

I ran for the shrubs and took cover, waited

fifteen minutes and figured he'd left. I peeked around my shoulder and almost fainted.

HE'D FOLLOWED ME TO THE BUSH AND WAS STANDING THERE, LOOKING INSIDE!!

I wiggled myself deeper into the undergrowth. That's when I heard his voice: "You in there? Yoo-hoo? Come out, we need to talk."

"You can't see me. I'm hidden."

"You're hidden, but I see you anyway."

"Bats can't see. I've heard about you guys—Halloween, witches, black cats, vampires, and 'blind as a bat.' Go away."

"We're not exactly blind, just a little nearsighted."

"So nearsighted that you walked right into a pond and almost drowned yourself."

"Look, George, it was an accident. I was about to die for a drink."

"Yeah, and you almost did, too. And my name's not George."

"Can we discuss this?"

"No. I don't associate with bats. My reputation around here is bad enough as it is."

He squeaked a little laugh. "Your reputation is 'bat' enough. Hee hee. I like that."

"Well, I don't like it, and it's not funny."

"Sorry. You're awfully sensitive."

"Who wouldn't be sensitive? Everybody thinks I'm a chickenhearted little mutt. If they saw me talking to you, they'd say I was batty."

"You're a chickenhearted little mutt?"

"Yeah, and I hate it."

"Hmmm. Bad deal. Maybe I can help."

"I don't need help from a bat. Just go away."

He said no more and I figured he took the hint and left. After waiting half an hour, I crawled out of the bush . . . and found him hanging upside-down from a branch. I was too surprised to speak.

He winked and grinned. "I figured you'd come out sooner or later. Ready to talk?" I darted back inside the bush and tried to hide. He followed me. "George, we have to talk, whether you like it or not."

"Go away."

"See, you saved my life."

"I'm sorry, it was an accident."

"Now I'm honor-bound to serve you. What do think of that, huh?"

I twisted my head around and stared at the ugly little creep. "Serve me? What does that mean?"

He propped himself up on one wing and let his gaze drift around. "Well, it's an old bat tradition.

You saved my life so I'm honor-bound to return the favor. I have no choice."

"I don't want a favor, and if I did, I wouldn't want it from a bat."

He shrugged. "We hear this all the time. What's wrong with bats? I don't get it."

"Everything's wrong with bats. You're creepy."

"That's what they say, but you know, I don't feel creepy. I feel like a normal, healthy American bat."

"You're creepy."

"Well, it doesn't matter. I have to do you a good deed, whether you like it or not. I'm Boris O'Bat, your faithful servant."

I edged toward him and offered a paw for him to shake. "I'm Drover. Nice to meet you . . . I guess." He reached out his wing but missed my paw. Like he'd said, he couldn't see very well.

"Okay, Drover, what can I do for you? Anything, just name it."

Well, what do you say to a bat? I told him the whole sad story about my cruel mother who wanted to throw me out of the yard and force me into honest work. When I was done, he gave his little shoulders a shrug. "Your mother's right. You need to leave home and find a job."

"Yeah, but I'm kind of short on ambition."

"You don't have plans, hopes, a dream?"

"Well . . . maybe one, but I hate to mention it. I've always thought it might be fun to be a handsome prince."

He beamed a smile and clapped his wings together. "Oh, that's perfect! This won't take long at all. See, there's a Handsome Prince School on the corner of Fifth and Congress, and I can take you right to it."

"Gosh, no fooling?"

He fluttered his wings and landed on the back of my neck. "Forward ever, backward never! Off we go to Handsome Prince School!"

So, with Boris O'Bat riding on my neck, I wiggled through the hole under the fence and we set off on our journey. Mom wouldn't have been proud to know that her son was hanging out with a bat, but at least she got her yard back.

CHAPTER TEN

Handsome Prince
School

Once we were outside the yard and in the alley, I asked Boris O'Bat for directions to the school.

He gave it some thought. "Let me do some calculations: left, right, up, down, sideways, backward. Let's go ... west."

"West puts us back in the yard."

"Oh, right. Sorry."

"Go right?"

"No, I said 'Oh, right.' Go north."

"North is left."

"That's right. Go north. Forward!"

This was a little confusing but I figured he knew what he was doing, so off we went, hiking up the alley to the north and toward the center of town. I started off in a trot, I mean, this was exciting. But after a while the heat started bothering me and I slowed to a walk. Then I stopped to rest.

"Boris?" No answer. "Are we almost there? Boris O'Bat?"

I heard a snorting sound. "Who called? Where am I?"

"Were you asleep?"

"Don't be ridiculous. Asleep? Well, maybe. Okay, I was asleep. Bats sleep during the day." He yawned. "What are we doing?"

"You're taking me to Handsome Prince School."

"Sure, got it, Handsome Prince School. Take the next right, go two blocks, then hang a left. That'll take us right to it. Wake me up when we get there."

Bats snore in their sleep. I didn't know that, but they do . . . or Boris did anyway. He made a lot of funny sounds, kind of like a miniature pig. I followed his directions and he slept the whole time. When I found myself standing in front of the Dixie Dog Drive-In Café, I began to wonder.

"Boris, wake up. We're here." He didn't answer, so I gave myself a shake that sent him tumbling to the ground.

He sat up and gave me an angry glare.

"What kind of camel are you, throwing off your passenger!"

"I'm not a camel, and this isn't the Handsome Prince School."

"Says who?"

"Says me. Read the sign."

He squinted his eyes. "Who makes these signs? It looks like a tree."

"It is a tree. You're looking in the wrong direction."

He turned to the left and squinted at a street lamp. "I can't make out the lettering. What does it say?"

"What are you, blind?"

"I told you, my eyes aren't so good. I've got glasses but I never wear them. They make me look like a freak."

"Well, since you're giving the directions, maybe you'd better put them on."

He scowled. "Promise you won't laugh?"

"Who could laugh? I think we're lost."

"Oh fiddle, we're not lost." Boris reached under his left wing and pulled out a little pair of spectacles with black rims. When he slid them on his nose, I laughed. They made his eyes look as big as baseballs. He said, "Dear Gussy, this isn't Handsome Prince School."

"I told you."

"Is this Congress Avenue?"

"It's Main Street."

He rolled his baseball-eyes around. "This is Austin, right?"

I couldn't believe it. "You're not only half-blind, you're a big faker, too. I'm going back home and I hope I never see you again."

I started walking away. He took off his glasses and followed me, hopping along on his wings. "Wait, let's talk. It was a little mistake. Are you going to hang a friend for making one little mistake? I hate wearing glasses."

"I'm not interested."

"Wait. Show me the Congress Avenue Bridge. I can find the school from there, honest."

"We don't have any bridges, because we don't have any rivers."

"No rivers? That can't be right. Austin has a river that goes right through the middle of town. It must be around here somewhere."

I stopped. "It's not around here somewhere because this is Twitchell, not Austin."

His jaw dropped. "Twitchell! I've never even heard of Twitchell."

"You're blind. Put on your glasses and take a look."

He jerked away. "The last time I wore them, you laughed and said I looked like a freak."

"I didn't say that, you said it."

"Well, you laughed."

"I won't laugh now, 'cause this isn't funny."

He reached under his wing and brought out his glasses. When he slid them on his nose, I had to bite my tongue to keep from going into stitches of laughter. I mean, the guy looked ridiculous.

He gazed out at the wide empty Main Street in front of us. He shook his head and heaved a sigh. "Oh brother! This isn't Austin. This isn't even *close* to Austin. This is Nothingsville! How did I get here?"

"Well, I can guess. You were too proud to wear your glasses, took a wrong turn, and missed Austin by five hundred miles."

"Five hundred miles! Are you serious?"

"You're in the Texas Panhandle."

His head slumped down on his chest. "The Panhandle! Oh brother. It snows up here, right? This is no place for a bat. I live under the bridge in Austin, and I've got to get home . . ." He cut his eyes at me. ". . . but I can't until I settle this business with you. And we have a problem."

"Yeah, you don't know the difference between the Dixie Dog and Handsome Prince School."

"Hey, cut me some slack, will you? I got the wrong town, that's all."

"Yeah, and that's enough." I stuck my nose in his face. "You're an ugly little bat. You look ridiculous in your glasses. I don't want any favors from you, and I'm going back home. Good-bye."

I walked away, leaving him alone on the curb. He yelled, "Hey, wait, come back here! I'm honor-bound, I can't go home until I return the good deed!"

I ignored him and walked on. I couldn't wait to tell Mom about the silly bat.

Looking for a Job

Abig surprise was waiting for me back at the yard. Mom didn't want to hear about Boris O'Bat or anything else. She wouldn't let me back in the yard and told me to go get a job. Her heart had turned to solid ice, and mine was broken.

Well, that settled it.

I spent the whole day looking for a job and you talk about tired, worn out, and discouraged! Every place I went, they laughed at me and said they didn't need a stub-tailed little mutt.

Okay, I went to one place, the Twitchell Livestock Auction, and had a job interview with the dog in charge of cow work. He was a blue heeler named Teaspoon, only he shortened his name to Spoon. I couldn't imagine how he got that name and he didn't say. Here's how it went.

SPOON: "I'm glad you stopped by, Drover. I'm looking for a few good dogs."

DROVER: "You probably wouldn't want me. I've got a stub tail."

SPOON: "No, that's fine. Most of your cowdogs have a docked tail."

DROVER: "Yeah, but mine looks ridiculous."

SPOON: "Son, we're hiring dogs, not tails. So you want a job, huh?"

DROVER: "My mother does."

SPOON: "Your mother wants a job?"

DROVER: "Yeah. For me."

SPOON: "Oh, one of those deals. Ha. Well, you're too old to be hanging around the house."

DROVER: "Actually, I'm still a kid, just big for my age."

SPOON: "You don't look so big."

DROVER: "That's what I mean. I'm kind of a runt."

SPOON: "My daddy used to say that if all four legs touch the ground, you're big enough to work."

DROVER: "Work? Ouch."

SPOON: "Something wrong?"

DROVER: "Oh, nothing. I've got a bad leg."

SPOON: "Which one?"

DROVER: "It varies."

SPOON: "I didn't notice you limping."

DROVER: "Sometimes it's okay, but then it quits me at the very worst times."

SPOON: "That's all right. Three legs'll do for this job. It ain't the Olympics. You ever worked around livestock?"

DROVER: "What's livestock?"

SPOON: "Cattle."

DROVER: "Oh, heck no. I'm scared of cows."

SPOON: "We can train you on the job."

DROVER: "I'm not very smart."

SPOON: "Good. In the long run, that helps."

DROVER: "And I've got no ambition. Zero."

SPOON: "Perfect. You're just the dog we've been looking for."

DROVER: "Uh oh, this old leg's getting worse."

SPOON: "You're hired, and you can start right now."

DROVER: "I can't walk!"

SPOON: "I'll get you a cane."

DROVER: "I'm allergic to wood."

SPOON: "It's fiberglass."

DROVER: "Help, murder! They're trying
to give me a job!"

Anyway, it was very discouraging, all those job interviews and all the rejections. Nobody wanted a mutt like me. I could have told 'em. I wouldn't have hired me either.

CHAPTER TWELVE

Mom Loses
Her Yard

It was one of the most discouraging days of my life. I had a feeling that Mom would want to hear all about it, so I headed back to the old homestead. I put on my best manners and tapped on the gate.

"Mom? You'll never guess who's here. Mom?" I tapped and tapped, then banged. Nobody came. Then I noticed a sign hanging on the gate.

WARNING!

This Yard Is Being Used As A
TOXIC WASTE DUMP!!
No Dogs Or Kinfolks Allowed!
Run Before It's Too Late!!!!!!!

Oh my gosh, what a disaster! They'd turned Mom's yard into a dump, and I just hoped she got out alive. Surely she did, but I didn't dare stick around to find out. I ran as fast as my legs would go, before the deadly fumes could get me.

Poor old Mom. She'd always loved her yard. Now she'd have to start all over again somewhere else. Gee, maybe I could find the new place and help her get settled in. Wouldn't she be thrilled?

Come to think of it, she might not be so thrilled. The last time I'd seen her, she'd been putting out pretty strong hints that she wanted me out. But wait, she'd want to hear about my first day of looking for a job, wouldn't she? Sure she would. I was still her son.

In a town of two thousand people and dogs, the odds of me finding her weren't so great, but I had nothing better to do. I walked up and down the alleys, calling, "Mom? Mother? Yoo-hoo, it's your child, your poor lost lonely child!"

I'd never thought about this before, but when you walk around town yelling "mother," every mother in town comes at a run, so that turned out to be not such a great idea and I gave it up. Mom would have to go to sleep that night, never knowing that her son had flunked his first job interview.

And maybe his last one, too. It's very discouraging when you put your very best into an interview and they still turn you down, just because you're a runt and have a stub tail and sneeze a lot and sometimes walk with a limp. This world can be a pretty cruel place.

By the time darkness fell, I had wandered to the south edge of town. If I kept walking, I would be out in the country and that was no place I wanted to be. I'd never been there, but I could imagine what I might find: lions, tigers, rippopotamuses, effanants, purple gorillas, giant lizards, and fifteen kinds of Night Monsters.

Who needed that? Not me.

I started back toward town, and that's when I noticed a bunch of trucks and tents sitting in a vacant field. And bright lights and music, nice music. It looked like a happy place, and after a day of heartbreak and failure, I found myself drifting toward it.

I'll be derned, it was a carnival. Right away, I remembered what Mom had told us kids about carnivals: stay away from 'em, 'cause there's nothing in a carnival for a nice little doggie.

Mom was right about most things, but you know what? Mom wasn't around to say no. Hee hee. And if they don't say no, it means yes.

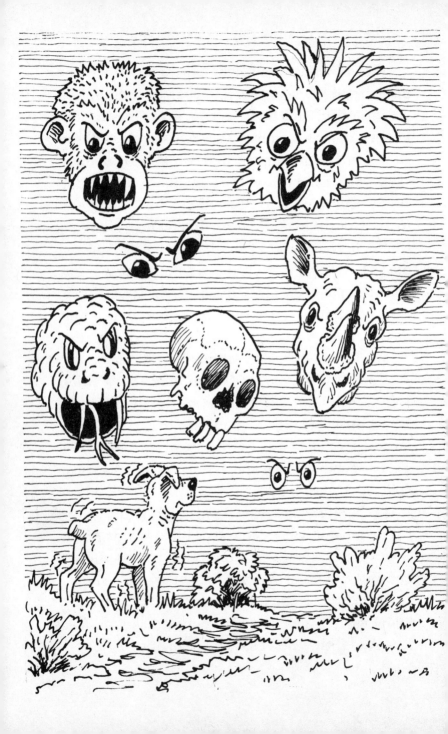

I have to confess something. Every once in a while I get an urge to be a naughty dog. I mean, I'd spent most of my life being a "nice little doggie," and what had it gotten me? Kicked out of my yard and out on the street without a job is what it had gotten me. And all of a sudden, I felt an urge to walk on the Wild Side.

I walked into the carnival. Boy, what an exciting place. Loud music, bright lights, kids eating pink stuffy stuck on a stiff . . . pink fluffy stuff on a stick, and people throwing baseballs at a target. Everybody was laughing and having fun, and all at once I forgot all my troubles and cares.

So there I was, walking and gawking my way through this amazing place, when I came to a tent with a big banner above the entrance. It showed this enormous snake, and I mean ENORMOUS, twenty-five-feet long and as big around as a tree. It had something in its mouth but you couldn't tell what it was, 'cause the snake had swallowed everything but two back legs.

I moved closer for a better look. It was pretty spooky. Oh, and there was a sign in big red letters that said, "DOG-EATING ANACONDA!!"

Just then, I heard a voice. "Pssssst! You there, come 'ere!"

I glanced around and saw a dog, peeking his head out of the tent. "Were you talking to me?"

"Yeah. Come 'ere."

He stepped out of the tent and I could see that he was one of those Doberman pinscher dogs— tall, thin, slick-haired, and pretty handsome but with a toothy smile. Big white teeth. I didn't care for his eyes. They were greenish and had a kind of cunning flash.

As I walked over to him, he seemed to be sizing me up. He nodded and said, "Yeah!"

"Hi there. I'm Drover. What's your name?"

"Everybody calls me Slick. How's it going, kid? You like the carnival? Having fun? What a place, huh?" He cocked his head to the side and narrowed his eyes. "Hey, what's this? You look sad. Don't tell me, let me guess. You're out on your own, first day in the world?"

"Well . . ."

"And things aren't going so great? The world's a big place and not so friendly? How'm I doing so far?"

"Well . . ."

"I knew it." He gazed up at the sky. "Let's see . . . bad day, discouraged, down in the dumps. Nobody's looking for another mutt, am I right?"

"Well . . ."

He moved closer and whispered, "They just don't understand who you really are, Rover. They just don't get it."

"It's *Drover,* with a *D.*"

"They don't understand that you're a little dog with big dreams that some day you'll become . . . help me here. What's your big dream?"

"Oh, I dream about bones sometimes."

His smile faded. "Don't tell me about bones. I'm talking about the Big Dream, the what's-deep-inside-you kind of dream, what you'd be if you could make a wish."

"Oh, that one."

"See? I knew it. Now, uh, help me here. What was that wish?" He cocked his ear and waited.

"Well . . . you'd probably think it was silly."

"Oh no, no, no! Look at all this, kid." He swept a paw toward the carnival. "It's one big dream in lights and music. That's our business, dreams."

"Oh. You work in the carnival?"

"Right. Now, you were saying?"

"Well . . . I've always thought it might be fun to be a handsome prince."

He flashed an ivory smile. "A handsome prince! Oh, perfect, great dream!"

Just then, another dog came out of the tent. This one was a little guy, one of those mutts with short legs and hair all over his face. He spoke to Slick. "You got one yet?"

Slick placed a paw on my shoulder. "Shorty, meet Rover, my new buddy."

"It's Drover, with a *D*."

"He wants to become a handsome prince!"

Shorty broke out in a cackling laugh. "Ha ha ha! That's a new one. Handsome prince! Ha ha ha ha!"

Slick glared at Shorty and used a hind leg to push him back into the tent. "Don't pay any attention to Shorty. He ain't too smart. Now, where were we? Oh yes, handsome prince." He glanced over both shoulders and whispered, "You won't believe this, kid, but this carnival has a training program for handsome princes."

"No fooling? But I thought Shorty said, 'That's a new one.'"

"What? Oh no, no, no, no. What he said was, 'I knew one.' See, he knew a dog who went through our Handsome Prince Program. Me, why, I've known dozens of them."

"Gosh, no fooling?"

"No fooling." He whispered behind his paw. "Dogs from all over Texas come here to learn Handsome Princing. This is the place, kid, believe me."

"I'll be derned."

He studied the claws on his right front foot. "So, uh, what do you say? Can we sign you up?"

"Well . . ."

"Hey, I'll make it easy. You don't even have to sign up. Just step inside the tent," he pushed open the tent flap, "and we'll start your training." He flashed his broad toothy smile.

"Well, I have a question."

His eyes drifted. "Great, we love questions."

"What's an anaconda?"

Going to College

Slick, the dog at the carnival, thought about my question. "An anaconda? Why, it's a kind of snake, a South American snake."

"Big?"

"Oh yes, they're big."

"Do they eat dogs?"

His smile wilted. "Now, why would you ask a question like that?"

"The banner in front of the tent. It says, 'Dog-eating Anaconda.'"

"Oh that! Ha ha! No, no, no, no. It's just an act, part of the show. We've got this dog, see, and he swallows snakes."

"Swallows snakes? That's yucky."

"I know, but we all have to make a living, right? This guy swallows snakes. Would I do it?

No. Would you do it? No. But there you go. It takes all kinds, kid."

"Yeah, but . . ."

"Oh, wait, I get it now. You thought . . . ha ha ha . . . you thought the snake swallows dogs?"

"Well, it says, '*Dog-eating Anaconda.*'"

"Ha ha ha! Kid, kid! You got everything backward. What it says, if I may paraphrase, what it says is, 'The dog eats the anaconda.' In other words, dog swallows snake, so we have *dog eating anaconda*. Get it?"

"No fooling? But the snake looks huge. How could a dog swallow such a big snake?"

"Well, uh, he's a big dog. I mean, what did you think, a little dog could swallow a big snake? No way. He's the biggest dog you ever saw, believe me."

"Boy, one little hyphen makes a big difference, doesn't it?"

"What hyphen are we talking about?

"The one between 'dog' and 'eating.' It's kind of confusing."

"You know, it is, and I'm glad you pointed that out. What a smart kid! So, what do you think? Are you ready to start your training?"

"Well, I guess so, if you're sure it's safe."

He glanced up at the clouds. "Safe? Rover, I've never felt safer in my whole life."

"It's Drover, with a *D*."

"Sure it is. Come on in, kid."

Wow. I couldn't believe my good luck! They were going to start my training right away. I went inside the tent, and Slick closed the flap and all at once it was kind of dark in there. Slick told me to sit down and he marched back and forth in front of me.

"Okay, kid, here's your first lesson. Think *handsome prince*. You're so handsome and so princely, you gotta act completely different, see what I mean? Normal behavior goes out the window, pow. You hold your nose high in the air, like this." He elevated his nose to a snooty angle. "And you don't even open your eyes."

"Gosh, how come?"

"Well, a handsome prince is important, right? Is he going to waste his time looking at the lowly masses? No, no, no, no. Think *handsome prince*. Think *important*. You got that?"

"Well, I guess so."

"Great. Try it. Nose up, eyes closed, now strut. Prance. Pick up those feet. Not bad. Remember, you're a very important handsome prince. Looking better. Doing good."

I pranced and strutted until I ran into a tent pole, and it sure hurt my nose. I opened my eyes and caught Slick trying to hide a laugh. I said, "It's hard to see when my eyes are closed."

"Practice. Where do you think handsome princes come from? They don't just fall off a load of turnips. Try it again."

I tried it again: snooty nose, snooty walk, snooty everything. It was beginning to feel more natural, and I did a whole lot better this time. Slick even said so. "Oh, this is amazing. Kid, you're a natural for this, and I'm being sincere."

"Gosh, thanks."

"In fact . . ." He struck a thoughtful pose. "You know what? We've got a show starting in about five minutes . . . crowd, audience, the whole deal. I'm going to let you walk across the stage, doing Handsome Prince. It'll be like your graduation. What do you think of that, huh?"

"Well, it's been my dream." I swallowed hard. "But I get nervous in front of a crowd."

"Oh bosh. They'll love you." He darted over to me and gave me a pat on the cheek. "Never forget, Rover, everybody loves a handsome prince. Sit down, relax. I'll be back in five minutes."

"It's Drover, with a *D*."

"You bet."

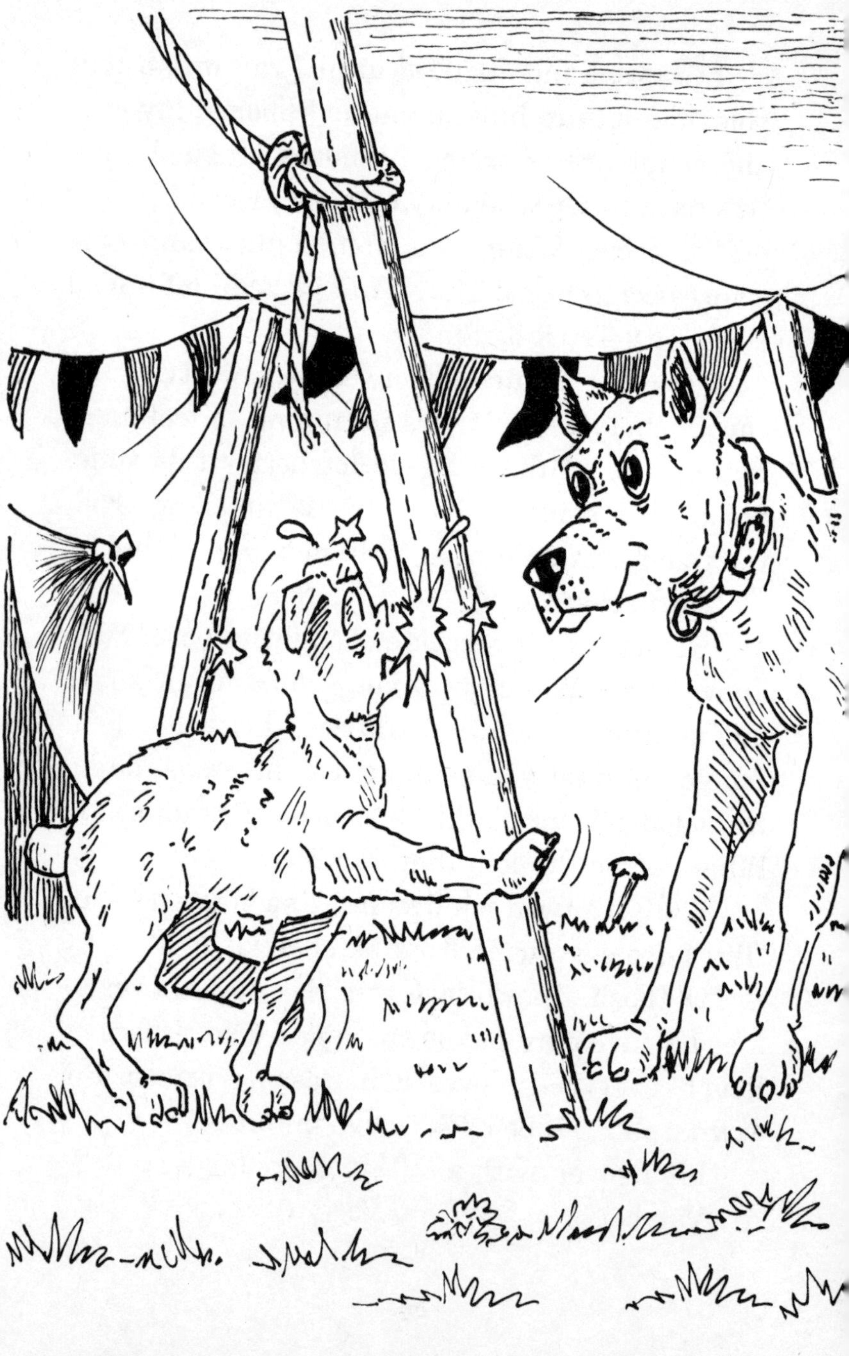

He hurried out and went to the other part of the tent where the crowd was gathering for the show. Boy, what a day. I just wished Mom could be there to see me. Wouldn't she be proud?

She'd be shocked, too. I don't think she ever thought I'd amount to much, but here I was, ready to graduate from college.

I sat down and waited for my big moment and listened as the noise of the crowd got louder and louder. I felt a little nervous but I knew that I could do it.

A bird flew into the tent. He swooped around a couple of times and I watched him. Birds are nice. It might be fun to be a bird. I tried flying once. I guess I mentioned that, but you know what? I think it was some kind of joke that Pete played on me, telling me that if I flapped my ears, I could fly. I flapped my ears and almost broke my nose off.

And you know what else? That wasn't a bird flying around inside the tent. It was a BAT and I even knew the guy. Boris.

He landed on the ground in front of me and said, "You are such a blockhead! I can't believe you're doing this."

"How can I be a blockhead? I'm about to graduate from college. Have you ever graduated from college, you ugly little bat? You're just jealous 'cause you'll never be a handsome prince."

He shook his head. "Do you know what this place is?"

"Heck yeah, it's the Handsome Prince School you couldn't find." I heard a roar of laughter from the crowd. "Isn't it?"

"It's a carnival. Didn't your mother ever warn you about carnivals?"

"Sure, but she's just a mom. What do they know?"

He stepped closer. "Listen, genius, in five minutes they're going to put you out on that stage. Do you know what's going to happen then? Huh?"

"Sure. I'll get my Handsome Prince Diploma."

"Wrong. You'll get eaten by a snake that's bigger than a tree!"

I giggled. "Tee hee hee. Oh that. I've already checked it out. See, they've got this big dog that swallows snakes. I'll get my diploma, and he'll do his show."

Boris moved right up into my face. "Oh yeah? Bad news. *You ARE the show.* They've set you up to be a hot dog for the biggest snake you ever dreamed of."

"Yeah, but Slick said . . ."

"March over there and peek out at the stage."

"Okay, I will, just to prove you're wrong." I went over to a flap in the tent, stuck my nose through the crack, and . . . GULP. I went back to Boris. "That can't be a snake."

"It's a snake."

"No snake is that big."

"It's an anaconda, and they eat things like sheep, goats, and meatheads."

"But Slick seemed like such a nice guy."

"Oh brother. Do you want to stay for the show and get eaten?"

Just then, we heard a voice. "Rover? Two minutes! Stand by!"

I looked down at my ugly little friend. "Oh, let's not wait."

"Well, glory be! Quick, run, follow me!"

He flew out the tent flap and I followed, just as fast as my . . . BAM! Drat the luck, the old leg went out on me. "Help, murder, oh my leg!"

Slick's voice boomed again. "Rover? One minute to show time!"

Boris came swooping back and crash-landed beside me. "Now what!"

"Well, this old leg just quit me, and oh, the pain!"

Boris's beady little eyes flicked back and forth.

"Pain? Okay, buddy, I'll show you pain." I couldn't believe what he did. He opened his jaws as wide as they would go and BIT me on my stub tail! "Now get up and run!"

Boy, that hurt. You wouldn't think a dinky little bat could cause much pain, but he did. It hurt so much, I almost forgot about the terrible pain in my leg. Anyway, I managed to run and followed Boris away from the carnival and back into town.

You probably think the snake ate me, but he didn't. Are you glad? I am.

CHAPTER FOURTEEN

The Park

We ran down alleys until we came to a park somewhere in the center of town. By then I was out of breath and had to stop and rest. Somehow my bad leg had stayed under me. I crawled under a bush and hid.

Boris still seemed to be in a bad mood. "Well, aren't you a piece of work."

"Thanks."

"You're a piece of work . . . like a flashlight without batteries. You were one minute away from being snake fodder."

"Let's talk about something else."

"I mean, the guy's name was *Slick* and you trusted him anyway!"

"He was friendly."

"He was a skunk, and not just an ordinary

skunk. He was a skunk working in a carnival! I can't believe you fell for it!"

"He said he would teach me to be a handsome prince."

"Well, guess what. He was a big fat liar. What are you doing in there?"

"I need a nap. It's the middle of the night and I'm worn out. You're not tired?"

He filled his lungs with air. "Not me, brother. Night's my time. While you sleep, I'll be out catching bugs."

"You eat bugs?"

"Of course. What did you think?"

"Well . . . I don't know. I thought bats drank blood, 'cause you're all vampires."

"Vampires!" He smacked his forehead with the tip of his wing. "How much of this can I take? For your information, I eat my weight in bugs every night. For your information, if it wasn't for bats like me, dogs like you would be crawling with mosquitoes. You like mosquitoes?"

"Not really."

"Then show some respect, would you?"

"Sorry I mentioned it."

"I'm going out for dinner. Good-bye!"

"Are you coming back?"

"No. I've finished my job. I'm gone." In the

blink of an eye, he was gone and hardly even made a sound. That's something I had noticed. Bats move through the air like a shadow and never even make a whisper of noise.

Well, I figured that was the last I would see of him and that was too bad, since I hadn't even thanked him for . . . well, I guess he saved my life. A shiver passed through my whole body as I remembered the snake. He was so huge, he could have eaten me in one gulp and wouldn't have even needed a toothpick.

I yawned and curled up in a ball, and the next thing I knew, it was broad daylight, noon or even later. I blinked my eyes against the bright sun and glanced around, trying to remember where I was. Oh yeah, the park. Handsome Prince School had turned into a complete bust, I'd almost been eaten by a snake, and I'd spent the night under a bush.

And just as I'd suspected, Boris O'Bat hadn't come back and that made me feel sad. Even though he'd been ugly and crabby, he'd turned out to be a pretty good friend. My only friend, come to think of it. Rats. My only friend in the whole world had quit on me.

I was about to cry when I looked up and saw something hanging from a branch overhead. It was brown and hanging upside down. Surely it couldn't be . . . but it was. Boris.

I had a hard time waking him up, had to shake him off the limb, and he woke up just as crabby as he'd been the night before. Or worse. Very crabby.

"Go away, will you!"

"I thought you'd gone back to Austin."

"I changed my mind."

"Oh goodie. I've got something to tell you."

He picked himself up and gave me a poisonous glare. "What? And it better be good."

"I had my heart set on being a handsome prince. Now I'm back to being a chickenhearted little mutt."

"You woke me up to tell me that?"

"Well, I felt sad and wanted to tell someone."

"And you picked me."

"Yeah, 'cause we're friends . . . I guess."

He gave his head a quick shake. "Great. Okay, do you want to hear the truth?"

"Is it good truth or bad truth?"

"It's truth truth."

"Uh oh, that's the worst kind."

"Are you ready to listen?"

"I don't think so." I covered my ears with my paws.

He moved closer and raised his voice. "You will never be a handsome prince."

"I can't hear you."

"Yes you can. I'm sorry, but you can't be a handsome prince because you're not handsome or princely."

"You've ruined my dream, and I'm going to cry."

"So cry. Get it out of your system. Wake me up when you're done."

I cried for five minutes and woke him up. When he yawned, I saw all those little spiky teeth in his mouth. No wonder my tail had hurt so much.

He said, "Well, did you get all the boo-hoo out of your system?"

"Some of it. I want to go home."

He rolled his eyes. "You just don't learn, do you? *Your mother doesn't want you back home.*"

"Maybe she's changed her mind."

"She hasn't changed her mind. She wants you to find your own place in the world. That's what every mother wants for her son."

"I'm going to cry again."

"Well, hurry up."

I cried for another five minutes and dried my eyes. "I guess you saved my life."

"Barely. You almost messed it up."

"Did I remember to say thank you?"

"As a matter of fact, no."

"Well, thanks. That makes us even. But how come you didn't go back to Austin?"

He heaved a sigh. "How can I go back to Austin and leave you in this condition?"

"What condition?"

"Helpless, hopeless, homeless, brainless, clueless. No job, no ambition. Son, you have to do something with your life!"

"Yeah, everybody keeps saying that, but . . . what?"

That pretty well killed the conversation. I guess he didn't have any answers either. We sat there for a long time, then Boris lifted his head. "Wait. I've got it. A song."

"What?"

"A song. I just thought of a song for you."

"Well, I'll bet it's pretty boring."

"Not the way I sing it. Listen to this."

I couldn't believe it. This ugly, scrawny little bat burst into song, right there in front of me.

CHAPTER FIFTEEN

I Never Knew Bats Could Sing

You Need a Dream

Now, listen to me, doggie, what I'm fixing to
    say.
The time has come for you to find a better
    way.
The course you've taken up to now just
    doesn't pay.
You need a dream
That you can reach.
Something simple.
I hate to preach.

Your momma tried to tell you, but you just
    didn't see.

She told you and told you that she wanted
    you to be
A reliable fellow who can stand on his feet.
You need a dream.
You can achieve.
Something simple.
I do believe.

Instead you've tried to hide behind your
    momma's fence,
Behaving like a mutt who didn't have good
    sense.
You've hoped that you'd become some kind of
    a handsome prince.
That's not a dream,
It's a mirage.
You'll never find it.
It's just a dodge.

So what does that leave and where do you
    stand?
Do you have any skills that could be in
    demand?
You can't continue living with your head in
    the sand.
So make your move.
Get off your duff.

Take a stand.
Show your stuff.

As for courage and brains, you're in short
supply.
But down where it counts, you're a decent
guy.
An honest dog can find a home and that's no
lie.
And there's your dream.
Go out and take it.
There's no excuse.
Go out and make it.

So there's you a dream that can be attained.
A dog needs a home like a flower needs rain.
And people need a dog they can love and
train.
Go find a child
And be his friend.
Stay by his side to
The bitter end.

He finished the song and took a bow. "Well,
there it is. What do you think?"

"I didn't know bats could sing."

"Hey, I'm from Austin, son, Music City on the

Rio Colorado. Any bat from Austin can sing like an angel."

"Well, it was pretty good, but I wouldn't say you sounded like an angel."

He scowled at me. "Did you listen to the message or were you asleep again? The song had a message for *you*."

"Yeah, I heard it: go find a home, make friends, all that stuff. That's easy to say, but I don't think I can do it."

"Will you at least try?"

"Well . . . I'm bashful. I get scared. And this old leg . . ."

He threw his wings into the air and stomped his feet in anger. "I can't believe this! Here you sit, quivering under a bush while life moves on without you. Do you think the world is going to come looking for you?"

I didn't have time to answer, which was good since I didn't have an answer. Just then we heard a sound, like a car door closing. I turned my head and saw that several cars . . . a bunch of cars had pulled up at the curb and people were getting out.

Boris squinted toward the sound. "What's going on over there?"

"I don't know, people in the park, I guess."

"Doing what?"

"I don't know. Put on your glasses and look for yourself."

He put on his glasses, and I tried not to laugh at how silly he looked. "Hey, they're carrying covered dishes. Food. Freezers of ice cream and lawn chairs. Somebody's cooking hamburgers. You know what? I think it's a picnic."

"And I'm going to cry. Nobody ever invites me to a picnic."

"Stop blubbering! This could be your big opportunity. Picnic, people. Somebody in that crowd needs a dog."

"Yeah, but not one like me. Nobody wants a little mutt with a stub tail."

"Get off your duff and go work the crowd!"

"I can't."

"If you won't do it for yourself, do it for me. Go find yourself a home . . ." He stepped right up into my face. ". . . *so I can go home!*"

"You don't need to scream."

"Of course I do. You're deaf, blind, and lazy. If somebody wasn't standing over you and screaming, you'd turn into a toadstool. Go work the crowd, move it!"

I took a few steps toward the crowd and stopped. "What'll I do?"

He let out a groan. "Am I a dog? Have I ever

been a dog? Do I know what a dog does to make himself irresistible? Whimper, look cute, look pitiful, roll over, shake hands, do a trick, chase a ball, beg."

"Yeah, but what if they hate dogs?"

He snatched off his glasses and pointed them at me. "Okay, buddy, that's enough! Do you want me to bite your tail again?"

"Not really. It hurt like crazy."

"Then beat it, go work the crowd. I'll be watching."

Well . . . he didn't leave me much choice. With a heavy heart, I trudged over to the picnic tables. I already knew how this was going to turn out: another big flop. No one was better at making flops than me.

A group of men stood around the charcoal cooker, talking about the weather and the wheat crop and pasture conditions, so I drifted over there and sat down. See? I knew it. They didn't even look at me. I was ready to call it quits and go home, only I didn't have a home anymore. My mother had kicked me out.

I sure felt discouraged, but before I could sneak off and hide, that bossy little bat swooped past and yelled, "Do a trick!"

A trick. Did I know any tricks? Maybe one.

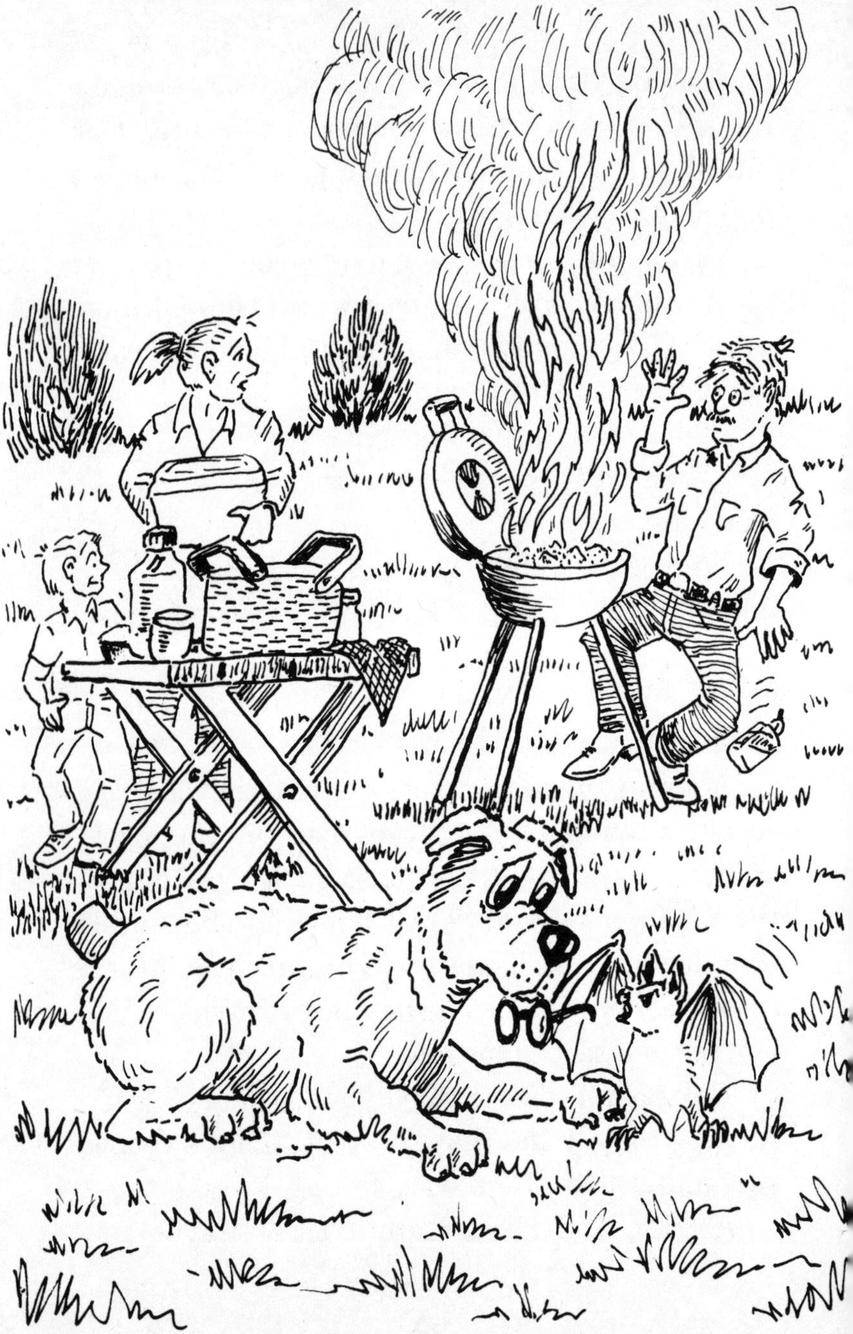

I'd learned how to shake hands, so I moved over to the group of the men and held up my paw and waited for someone to notice and shake my hand and laugh and say I was cute and take me home.

I stood there for two whole minutes and got no takers. Just what I figured. They hated dogs, every last one of them, and they hated me most of all. But before I could sneak off, Boris swooped past again and yelled, "Scratch that man on his leg!"

"What? Splash on his leg? I don't think that's a good idea." But Boris had already disappeared. I studied all the legs in front of me, about twenty-five of them. Well, I thought to myself, here goes.

The guy whose leg I splashed didn't notice it for a minute, until he felt water in his shoe, and when he whirled around, it wasn't to shake hands. He screeched and chased me under a picnic table.

Boy, that one backfired. The rest of the men howled with laughter, but the one I'd splashed kept shooting me angry looks. I was ready to give up, but the bat landed in the grass nearby.

"What was that all about?"

"I did what you said. I splashed on his leg."

His eyes rolled up to the sky. "I said SCRATCH on his leg! Scratch on his leg to get his attention, then shake hands."

"Oh. I wondered about that. Well, I got his attention."

"Oh brother!"

"Can I leave now? Everybody hates me."

"No. Stay and work the crowd." He put on his glasses and pointed to a group of children romping around in the grass. "Aha, kids. That's the ticket. Everybody loves a dog who plays with kids."

"What if they make fun of my tail?"

"They won't make fun of your tail. They're sweet, they're nice."

"They're noisy."

The bat puffed himself up and hissed, "Well, too bad. Get over there and play ball with the kids."

"I'm not very athletic."

"I don't care."

"I don't know how to play ball."

"Figure it out. Go!"

Drat. It sure sounded like a lot of trouble. Oh well. I wandered over to the group of kids who were throwing a little rubber ball around. One of them saw me and . . . gosh, he smiled and seemed glad to see me.

"Hi puppy. You want to play ball?"

Oh sure. Ball. How fun.

"Okay, I'll throw the ball and you go fetch." He gave the ball a toss. "Fetch! Fetch!"

Fetch? That was a new one on me. It sounded like "catch" but I couldn't see any way of catching a ball he'd thrown off in the distance. It was confusing. He kept looking at me, waiting for me to do something. Well, maybe "fetch" meant shake hands, so I offered him a paw.

He laughed. "No, doggie, don't shake. Fetch!"

The pressure was really on. I switched to the other foot and gave him my left front paw.

"No, no. Fetch! Fetch!"

Roll over? Okay, it seemed like a lot of trouble, but maybe I could do it. I rolled over . . . twice, in fact, but when I looked around, they were all gone, chasing after the ball. I thought about romping around with them, but you know, romping is a lot of work. I'd never been real keen about romping and what I needed was a nap.

There was some nice shade beneath the picnic tables, so I headed in that direction, hoping Boris O'Nuisance wouldn't notice. But of course he did, and here he came.

"Now what?"

"I flunked that one, too."

"They wanted you to chase the ball and bring it back. That's fetching."

"Oh, I wondered. Well, it's too late now."

"Get back out there and play with the kids!"

"I'm exhausted."

"You're a lazy slug, is what you are."

"Maybe a nap'll bring me around, just a couple hours."

He rolled his beady little eyes. "Fifteen minutes. I'll be back to wake you up."

I hoped he'd forget about me. No, he wouldn't forget. He'd be back to pester me again, but maybe a rest in the shade would restore my energy. I'd never dreamed that looking for a home could be so much trouble.

CHAPTER SIXTEEN

A Hero Finds a Home

I parked myself in the shade under one of the tables and watched all the activity. The men were cooking hamburgers, and the smoke smelled good. Several of the ladies set cakes on the tables and opened up three freezers of homemade ice cream. I was tempted to go on a begging expedition, but what if they yelled at me and chased me away?

Besides, ice cream is so cold, it hurts my teeth.

So I just laid there in the shade, watched all the action, and flicked my ears to keep the flies from biting. You wouldn't think that flicking your ears would make you tired, but it did. I had almost dozed off when a woman walked past the table and something fell right between my front paws. I leaned my nose toward it and gave it a sniff.

It appeared to be some kind of jewelry. A necklace or something. I wondered if it might be good to eat. Nope. It was hard and had no taste and I spit it out. Then I noticed a group of ladies walking around the picnic area, with their eyes on the ground. Huh. Maybe they were looking for something.

One of them said, "Sally May, it's here somewhere."

And the lady named Sally May said, "It was my grandmother's favorite necklace. If I've lost it, I'll just die! Loper, would you come help me look for my necklace?"

I'll be derned. She'd lost a necklace. What a coincidence. I had one right between my front paws. After a couple of yawns, I took a closer look at the necklace. Hmmm. Necklace? Gosh, maybe the necklace they were looking for was the one between my paws. Well, surely they would see it sooner or later.

Several people walked past but none of them noticed the jewelry, and I even barked once to get their attention. It wasn't much of a bark, more of a grunt, but they should have heard it.

Then an interesting idea popped into my head.

If they were looking for the necklace between my paws, maybe I could pick it up in my mouth and take it to the lady named Sally May. That would be a noble thing to do, and she would be grateful. Maybe she'd give me a burger. Or a piece of cake. I love cake.

But the afternoon sun was glaring down, and it had gotten awfully hot. To deliver the necklace to her, I would have to jack myself up to a standing position, bend down, pick up the necklace in my mouth, and walk all the way over to her in the hot sun.

Whew! Just thinking about it made me tired, and then my old leg went to throbbing and that pretty well killed the idea.

The search party grew larger, until the whole picnic came to a stop. Everybody was walking around, searching the ground. The hamburgers burned, the ice cream melted, and Sally May dropped into a lawn chair and buried her face in her hands. The others stood around, wearing long faces and shaking their heads.

This was really sad, and I even started sniffling. A family treasure, lost at a picnic. It was just a pity they hadn't looked between my paws. Heck, it was right there in plain sight. Anybody could see it.

A big tear had just slid down my cheek when I heard a fluttering sound, and Guess Who landed beside me. He had his glasses on and his eyes reminded me of grapefruits. I wanted to laugh but didn't. It would have made him mad.

"Take the necklace to the lady."

"Me?"

"You."

"It's not mine."

"That's the point."

"What if they think I stole it?"

"Take the necklace to the lady!"

"My leg's tearing me up."

He lifted his lips and showed me his spike teeth. "You've got a choice here. I can either chew off your tail or both ears."

"You said you ate bugs, not tails."

"Hurry up."

"I don't like you."

"Ears or tail?"

"You're a bossy, ugly, crabby, grapefruit-eyed little creep of a bat." He opened his jaws and moved toward my tail. "Okay, okay. I'm going."

"You ought to be ashamed of yourself."

"Yeah, but I'm not. If I die of heat stroke, it'll be your fault." I picked up the necklace in my jaws and walked out into the broiling sun. I almost

114

fainted from the heat, but somehow I dragged myself across the grass to the chair where Sally May was sitting.

I stood there, waiting. She didn't notice. Nobody noticed. Well, I'd done my best. I turned and was about to go back to the shade when someone said, "Oh, look. That dog found your necklace!"

A gasp went up from the crowd and things happened so fast, it was all a blur. The next thing I knew, I was sitting in Sally May's lap and she was laughing and hugging my neck. And everyone around us was smiling and patting me on the head. Gee, it was almost like I'd become a hero or something. Or even a handsome prince.

It was about the most exciting thing that had ever happened to me, and it got even better, 'cause Sally May noticed that I didn't have a collar and asked her husband if they could take me home to their ranch. He grunted something about how I didn't look much like a ranch dog, but he finally said okay.

And that's how I ended up on the ranch, by doing good deeds and being a brave little doggie. The bravery didn't last long, but it was there when I needed it.

While the crowd ate their lunch, I sat in the shade and watched. Boris landed beside me and

gave me a grin. "What did I tell you? You worked the crowd and look what it got you."

"Yeah, I still can't believe it. They didn't even care that I'm a stub-tailed little mutt."

"See? There you go. It's like I said, a good heart trumps everything else. An honest dog can always find a job."

"Yeah, but if you hadn't been here to nag and threaten, I would have messed it up."

He shrugged and flashed a smile. "Well, the math worked out, didn't it? You pulled me out of a pond, and I helped you find a job. That's why we all need friends."

"I kind of wish you could stay around. I'm just starting to like you."

"Nope, got to go. Austin's calling my name." He cocked his ear and listened. "Yep, there it is: 'Boris, come home!' Any messages for the legislature?"

"What does that mean?"

"It's a joke, never mind. Well, congratulations on finding a home. They look like nice people."

"Thanks for your help. You're a pretty nice bat, but can you find your way back to Austin?"

He flashed a grin and pointed to his bug eyes. "Oh yeah. This time, I'm wearing my specs. The Panhandle's okay, but I don't want to be here come winter. Snow? I hate the stuff." He threw his wings around my neck and gave me a hug. "Be good, be brave, and eat your spinach!"

"Spinach?"

Before I had a chance to tell him that dogs don't eat spinach, he spread his wings and flapped away. He flew around in a couple of circles, then set a course straight south ... toward Austin.

I guess that business about eating spinach was another joke. Sometimes it takes me a while to catch on.

Well, there's My Secret Life. It wasn't so bad, was it? And it had a happy ending. I got me a home on a nice ranch and found some friends: Hank and Pete and J. T. Cluck the rooster, and Loper and Sally May and Slim Chance the cowboy. Six months later, Little Alfred was born. He grew up to be a noisy little boy, but we get along okay. When the noise gets unbearable, I duck into the machine shed.

Mom was thrilled when she heard about my new job, but you know that deal about the Toxic Waste Dump? It was just a trick. She fooled me.

Oh well. It's turned out nice and I love happy endings. As Hank would say, "This case is closed."

Have you read all
of Hank's adventures?

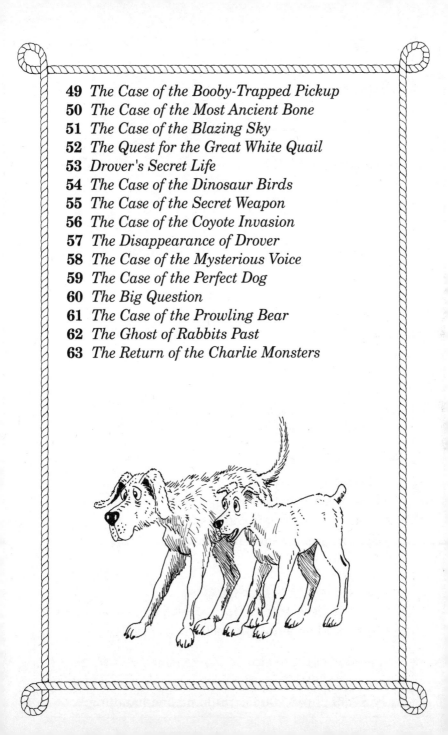

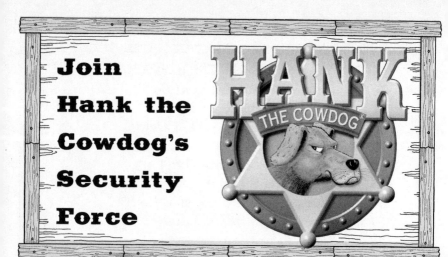

Join Hank the Cowdog's Security Force

Are you a big Hank the Cowdog fan? Then you'll want to join Hank's Security Force! Here is some of the neat stuff you will receive:

Welcome Package
- A Hank paperback
- An Original (19"x25") Hank Poster
- A Hank bookmark

Eight digital issues of *The Hank Times* with
- Lots of great games and puzzles
- Stories about Hank and his friends
- Special previews of future books
- Fun contests

More Security Force Benefits
- Special discounts on Hank books, audios, and more
- Special Members-Only section on website

Total value of the Welcome Package and *The Hank Times* is $23.99. However, your two-year membership is **only $7.99** plus $5.00 for shipping and handling.

☐ Yes I want to join Hank's Security Force. Enclosed is $12.99 ($7.99 + $5.00 for shipping and handling) for my **two-year membership**. [Make check payable to Maverick Books.]

Which book would you like to receive in your Welcome Package? (#   ) any book except #50

_____

BOY or GIRL

YOUR NAME   (CIRCLE ONE)

_____

MAILING ADDRESS

_____

CITY   STATE   ZIP

_____

TELEPHONE   BIRTH DATE

_____

E-MAIL   (required for digital Hank Times)

Send check or money order for $12.99 to:

Hank's Security Force
Maverick Books
PO Box 549
Perryton, Texas 79070

DO NOT SEND CASH. NO CREDIT CARDS ACCEPTED.
Allow 2–3 weeks for delivery.
Offer is subject to change.

The following activity is a sample from *The Hank Times*, the official newspaper of Hank's Security Force. Please do not write on this page unless this is your book. Even then, why not just find a scrap of paper?

For more games and activities like this one, as well as up-to-date news about upcoming Hank books, be sure to check out Hank's official website at **www.hankthecowdog.com**!

Hank's PicWords

Hank and his friends made some PicWords that need to be unscrambled. Use the character name or item illustrated below. Then subtract the letters indicated from each name or word. Add what's left over together and the PicWord will be solved. Good luck!

$$\left(\text{[face]} - se\right) + \left(\text{[cat]} - pe\right) =$$

$$\left(\text{[stamp]} - amp\right) + \left(\text{[dog]} - drr\right) =$$

$$\left(\text{[big]} - ig\right) + \left(\text{[dog head]} - h\right) + \left(\text{[ear]} - a\right) =$$

$$\left(\text{[dog head]} - ank\right) + \left(\text{[switch off]} - n\right) + \left(\text{[cat]} - te\right) =$$

Photogenic Memory Quiz

We all know that Hank has a "photogenic" memory—being aware of your surroundings is an important quality for a Head of Ranch Security. Now you can test your powers of observation.

How good is your memory? Look at the illustration on the following page and try to remember as many things about it as possible. Then turn the page and see how many questions you can answer.

1. Was Drover looking up or down?

2. How many letters was the postman holding? 1, 2, or 3?

3. Was the flag up on the mailbox? Yes or No?

4. How many "little" thought bubbles were there? 2, 3, or 4?

5. Was the mailman's bag on his left or right shoulder?

6. How many of the "big" Drover's paws cold you see? 2, 3, 4, or 5?

Rhyme Time

What would happen if Hank the Cowdog quit his job as Head of Ranch Security and began to look for other jobs? What jobs could he do?

When Hank runs into Rip and Snort, the coyote brothers, they call him Hunk. Make a rhyme using the name Hunk that would relate to the jobs described below.

Example: Hunk (Hank) could go to school and not study to do this: HUNK FLUNK

1. Hunk becomes a professional basketball player.

2. Hunk gets a vacant lot and fills it with old cars and iron scraps.

3. Hunk impersonates a black-and-white animal.

4. Hunk takes care of his nieces and nephews.

5. Hunk is a test subject for a machine that reduces things.

6. Hunk becomes a leaky boat.

7. Hunk goes to camp and gets a new bed.

8. Hunk retires to the Emerald Pond.

9. Hunk invents a new chocolate chip that is very, very thick.

10. Hunk becomes a car's luggage storage space.

Answers:

1. Hunk DUNK
2. Hunk JUNK
3. Hunk SKUNK
4. Hunk UNC
5. Hunk SHRUNK
6. Hunk SUNK
7. Hunk BUNK
8. Hunk STUNK
9. Hunk CHUNK
10. Hunk TRUNK

Eye-Crosserosis

I've done it again. I was staring at the end of my nose and had my eyes crossed for a long time. And you know what? They got hung up—my eyes, I mean. I couldn't get them uncrossed. It's a serious condition called Eye-Crosserosis. (You can read about the big problems Eye-Crosserosis caused me in my second book.) This condition throws everything out of focus, as you can see. Can you help me turn the double letters and word groupings below into words?

Insert the double letters into the word groupings to form words you can find in my books.

DD	RR	OO	SS	EE	TT
PP	LL	ZZ	UU	DD	GG

1. MIOR _____

2. PUY _____

3. BIROG _____

4. MNBEAMS _____

5. VACM _____

6. SALE _____

7. BUARD _____

8. GRN _____

9. MIING _____

10. CALE _____

11. DOIE _____

12. WAACE _____

Photo Courtesy of Western Horseman Magazine

John R. Erickson,
a former cowboy, has written
numerous books for both
children and adults and is
best known for his acclaimed
Hank the Cowdog series. He
lives and works on his ranch
in Perryton, Texas, with his
family.

Gerald L. Holmes
has illustrated numerous
cartoons and textbooks in
addition to the *Hank the
Cowdog* series. He lives in
Perryton, Texas.

Shawn Tevis Photography